THE ADVENTURES OF IGGY THE ROCK

By **Jennifer Malyka**

Illustrated by Angel Dela Pena

ISBN
978-1-4828-8056-4 (sc)
978-1-4828-8057-1 (e)

Print information available on the last page.

To order additional copies of this book, contact
Toll Free 800 101 2657 (Singapore)
Toll Free 1 800 81 7340 (Malaysia)
www.partridgepublishing.com/singapore
orders.singapore@partridgepublishing.com

04/03/2019

PARTRIDGE

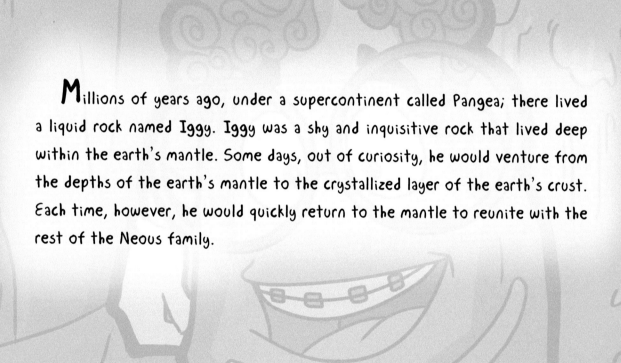

Millions of years ago, under a supercontinent called Pangea; there lived a liquid rock named Iggy. Iggy was a shy and inquisitive rock that lived deep within the earth's mantle. Some days, out of curiosity, he would venture from the depths of the earth's mantle to the crystallized layer of the earth's crust. Each time, however, he would quickly return to the mantle to reunite with the rest of the Neous family.

One day, Grandpa Neous decided to tell his grandson about the journey that lay before him. Grandpa Neous told Iggy that as a member of the Neous family, he would need a strong mind and solid character in order to endure the next stage of his life. Iggy asked curiously, "What stage?" to which Grandpa Neous replied, "Iggy Neous, you know how you like to journey to the earth's crust only to quickly return to the mantle? Well, one day you will go to the earth's crust and stay there for a very long time." "No way," replied Iggy. Grandpa continued, "You will go to the earth's crust and change into a solid rock but that's not the only changes, you are going to go through.

While on the earth's surface, you will combine with other elements and minerals to become different types of rocks. On your journey, you will meet all types of colorful and unique rocks. Some of them older than you and some of them younger than you but all of them will contribute to your development." Iggy listened intently as he did not know how to respond to all that was being told by Grandpa Neous. Iggy then asked, "Why do I have to go through this Grandpa? I want to stay here with you and the rest of the family." Grandpa replied, "All real rocks must go through these stages, but don't you worry because at the end you will return right here for yet another journey. I must warn you, Iggy, it will be challenging for you at times but with a good heart and good company you should have a rewarding journey. Always remember Iggy, that you are a part of the **Igneous** family.

Later on that day, Iggy, decided to take a trip to the earth's crust just to prepare for his future journey. Surprisingly, Iggy did not know that his journey had actually begun. This time instead of floating near the ocean vents, oddly, Iggy decided to go near the huge towering volcanoes that always fascinated him. While floating within the mantle the magma's viscosity began to decrease and its pressure began to increase, causing Iggy to lose track of his direction. Iggy was prevented from returning where he started but he still tried with all of his strength to swim against the currents of the magma. Exhausted of his energy, Iggy was finally forced to the opening of a volcano vent where all of a sudden he was hurled upwards into the vast unknown of earth.

For awhile, Iggy lay motionless as he slowly began to solidify in the process known as **crystallization**. Immediately, Iggy felt how cold the earth's surface was in comparison to the earth's mantle. He also noticed unique structures and life forms that did not exist in the earth's mantle as well. There were towering trees everywhere with all sorts of colorful animals and plants. Every part of the earth's surface seemed to enchant Iggy and when he tried to move, that's when he realized that he could not move as in the earth's mantle. That's also when he heard a laugh from a neighboring rock. "This must be your first journey," said a conglomerate rock. "Let me introduce myself, my name is Seddie and right now you are on this huge landmass called Pangea. As you can see it is nothing like the dark, hot vastness of the earth's mantle.

Above the Earth's crust, there is a sky that rains a cool liquid that is needed to sustain all living things up here. A lot of this liquid can be found in a place called Panthalassa which has all kinds of colorful creatures. Hey, you might even get a chance to visit there sometime during your journey. Oh yeah, just in case you are wondering, that gigantic bright light up there is called the sun and when it goes away, it looks just like the mantle up here. The only difference is that a smaller light comes out that shines a little light in the darkness. This has been going on for eons", continued Seddie.

"Life is always changing here, one minute here and the next minute you will probably be carried on to some other part of Pangea," stated Seddie. "How long have you been here?" asked Iggy. "I've been here for thousands of years but I will probably begin the next stage of the rock cycle any time soon." As the days became months and the months became years, Iggy and Seddie would spend most of their time talking about Pangea and Panthalassa. Also with the passing years, Iggy began to notice that he was becoming smaller and smaller as if bits and pieces of him were being carried with the wind. When he told Seddie about his sudden weight loss, she simply stated that he was going through a process called **weathering.**

She explained that with weathering, the wind would cause bits and pieces of him to be carried away and that those bits and pieces of him were called **sediments.** He could not believe her when she told him that those bits and pieces would go on to become a new type of rock. Iggy was relieved that he had a friend like Seddie to comfort him during his growing pains, although this relief would be short —lived. One day, after Pangea shook hard for a very long time, Seddie could be heard saying, "Farewell Iggy, it was nice knowing you kid!" For Seddie had fallen into a deep abyss created after the quake and so she was no longer around to comfort him.

Life as Iggy knew it continued but without the friendship of Seddie. One day, as Iggy was gazing at the sky, a tremendous wind carried him to a distant part of what was once known as Pangea. He seemed to have traveled for ages before being **deposited** in what was now known as Gondwana.

In Gondwana, Iggy found himself in tight conditions with other sediments around his size. With time, all of the sediments began to form a large rock by sticking together in a process known as **lithification**. Iggy was now a part of a much bigger **sedimentary rock.** Each of the sediments contributed to the rock but each maintained their own uniqueness. They even formed a rock group called "The Sediments". The Sediments had a jolly good time talking about the changes going on around them and singing songs like "Solid as a Rock". Yet, Iggy's heart yearned to be with his Grandpa Neous.

Once again, time passed, with some of the sediments being carried away and others staying apart of their bigger rock. Just as Iggy thought he would remain there forever, he was separated from the sediments and free-falling into the great below. He yelled, " I'll be seeing you." before falling into the darkness of the great below. As he descended further underground, he was slowly transformed into a different type of rock. The pressure of the above layers had changed Iggy into a beautiful **metamorphic rock.**

With time, Iggy felt at home in his new environment as a metamorphic rock.   Even though he had enjoyed his life above the ground, he still missed those earlier years when he was a baby rock playing with the Neous family members. He missed those wise talks he use to have with his Grandpa Neous about skipping some stages of the rock cycle before beginning a new journey. Surprisingly, Iggy did not know that he was about to complete the last stage of his first journey. As he descended farther into the inner parts of the earth and as the temperature increased, Iggy began to dissolve into liquid rock. And even though it had been hundreds of thousands of years since Iggy had been in the mantle, he remembered its parts like yesterday.

When he finally arrived near his home of yesteryears, he found his Grandpa Neous. With a warm greeting, he shouted, "I missed you Grandpa Neous." Grandpa replied, "So you're back from your first rock cycle journey, how was it?" Iggy began to tell his grandpa about all that he had experienced and the rocks that he befriended. He talked about the beauty of Pangea and Gondwana and the different types of plants and animals that lived up on the surface. He talked about the Big light and the Small light and his role in storing minerals for future use. His Grandpa Neous was very proud of him because he had left as a baby liquid rock and came back as Iggy, an experienced member of the Neous family.

Printed in the United States
By Bookmasters